DISNEP PRESENTS A PIXAR FILM

p

Lightning McQueen revved his engine and glanced across at his rival Chick Hicks. They were on the starting line at the biggest race of the season – the Dinoco 400.

Also at the start was The King, the current champion. This would be his last ever race, which meant the lucrative Dinoco sponsorship was up for grabs.

VA-RROOM!

With a screech of burning rubber, the cars sped off down the track. McQueen burst past Chick at the first bend. Angrily, Chick bumped McQueen off the track. The rookie soon got back into the race, only to face a huge pile-up caused by the cheating Chick. But McQueen had his own way of avoiding the crash and shot into the lead!

When McQueen pulled into the pits, he filled up with gas but ignored his crew's advice to change tyres. He increased his lead, but it was risky. In the last lap his back tyres blew. Chick and The King drew level with him just as he limped across the finishing-line.

It was too close to call! While McQueen waited for the race results, he posed for the reporters, pushing his pit crew aside. Furious, they quit on the spot. Then the announcement came.

"Ladies and gentlemen, for the first time in Piston Cup history we have a three-way tie!"

A tie-breaker race would be held in California in one week. McQueen groaned. He had been so sure he had won.

McQueen ordered his truck, Mack, to drive through the night to California. He promised Mack that he would stay up with him, but he soon fell asleep. Many hours later, a gang of cars pulled alongside the exhausted truck and began bumping him for a laugh. Mack swerved dangerously and McQueen was thrown out of the trailer on to the Interstate.

McQueen woke up to oncoming traffic! He thought he saw
Mack pull off the Interstate and quickly followed, but it wasn't
Mack and he was lost. Then he noticed a police car on his tail.

ANG! BANG! BANG! The Sheriff's exhaust backfired.
"He's shooting at me!" cried McQueen.

He tore off up the main street of a small town, destroying
everything in his path. He ended up dangling helplessly
between two telegraph poles.

"Boy, you're in a heap of trouble," said the Sheriff.

The next morning McQueen woke up to see a cheery tow truck grinning at him from the gates of an impound lot.

"Hi, there! My name's Mater" he said. "Welcome to Radiator Springs!"

At that moment, the Sheriff arrived to escort McQueen to court. The judge, Doc Hudson, wanted to kick McQueen out of town, but Sally, the attorney, had a better idea; McQueen couldn't leave until he had repaired the town's damaged road.

Reluctantly, McQueen set to work pulling Bessie, the enormous road-surfacing machine. When he heard a radio report that Chick was already in California practising for the tie-breaker race, he pulled Bessie as hard and fast as he could. A couple of hours later, he announced that the road was finished. But it was a total mess.

"Now it matches the rest of the town," sneered McQueen.

Doc was furious. He
decided to settle matters
with a race.

"If you win, you go and I
fix the road. If I win, you do
the road my way," he said.

Out at the dirt track, McQueen took
a quick lead. But he misjudged a tricky bend and wiped out!
Mater hauled the humiliated McQueen out of the ditch and
he was sent back to work. By the next morning Radiator
Springs had a patch of beautifully surfaced road.

McQueen was tired and filthy. Red, the fire engine gave him a refreshing spray down. Then Sally thanked McQueen for his hard work by letting him stay at her motel instead of the impound.

That night, Mater took McQueen tractor tipping and showed off his backward driving skills. McQueen said if he got the Dinoco sponsorship deal he'd get Mater a ride in their helicopter.

"You're my best friend," said Mater.

McQueen smiled. He had never had a best friend before.

The next morning, Sally gave McQueen a full tank of petrol. He could have sped out of town, but he went for a drive with Sally up the mountain instead. She stopped outside a deserted motel.

"This used to be the most popular stop on Highway 66," sighed Sally. She talked about the old days before they built the Interstate, when Radiator Springs was a bustling town.

Later that afternoon, McQueen was helping the town to catch a stray tractor when he spotted Doc at the dirt track. Since arriving in Radiator Springs, McQueen had learnt that Doc had once been a famous racing car champion himself.

McQueen watched in amazement as Doc manoeuvred effortlessly around the tricky corner that had given the rookie so much trouble.

McQueen followed Doc back to his office. He needed to know what had happened to end Doc's career as the Fabulous Hudson Hornet. He had won three Piston Cups in the 1950s.

"How could a car like you quit at the top of his game?" asked McQueen.

"You think I quit? They quit on me," Doc replied bitterly. Doc told him how he had nearly been ruined in a crash. When he recovered, he found he had been replaced by a rookie – a rookie like McQueen.

By the following morning, McQueen had finished his work, but he couldn't leave yet. He visited all the shops in town and became the best customer they had seen in years. He treated himself to a new set of tyres and a shiny new paint job.

Inspired by the new road, the shopkeepers had been sprucing up their shops. That evening they turned on their neon signs just like in the good old days. Everyone cruised happily up and down. It was all so perfect...

… until a wall of headlights approached the town.

"We have found McQueen!" boomed a voice from a helicopter. It was a gang of reporters! Mack was there to take McQueen to the big race. Fighting his way through the crowds, McQueen found Sally. He didn't know what to say.

"I hope you find what you're looking for," Sally told him. Then she disappeared into the crowd.

As Mack pulled out of town with McQueen on board, all the reporters followed, but one stopped to thank Doc before joining them. Sally was stunned. Doc was the one who had told them where to find McQueen!

"It's best for everyone," said Doc.

"Best for everyone, or best for you?" challenged Sally.

"I didn't even get to say goodbye to him," Mater said sadly.

The lights were turned off and everyone went home silently. Everyone, that is, except Doc. He felt ashamed as he realized how much McQueen had done for their town.

A few days later, McQueen found himself speeding around the Los Angeles International Speedway in the biggest race of his life. But his heart wasn't in it. He kept thinking about the new friends he had left behind in Radiator Springs. Suddenly, he heard a familiar voice over his radio.

"You can win this race with your eyes shut!" It was Doc! All of his Radiator Springs friends had come to be McQueen's pit crew!

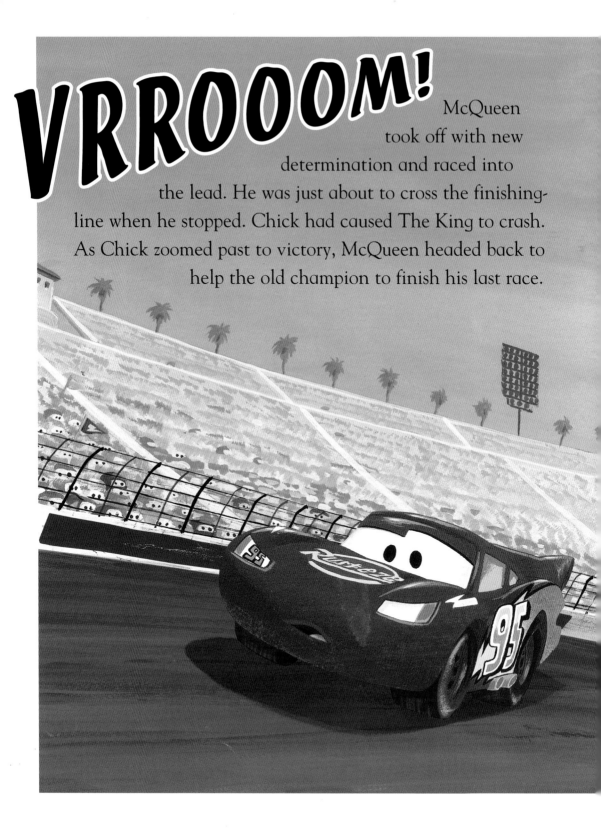

VRROOOM!

McQueen took off with new determination and raced into the lead. He was just about to cross the finishing-line when he stopped. Chick had caused The King to crash. As Chick zoomed past to victory, McQueen headed back to help the old champion to finish his last race.

The crowd went wild as McQueen pushed The King across the finishing-line!

Even though McQueen hadn't won, Tex, the owner of Dinoco, asked him if he wanted to be the new face of Dinoco. McQueen decided to stay with his sponsor, Rust-eze, but he did ask Tex for one small favour...

Back at the Wheel Well Motel, Sally looked out over the valley. Suddenly, she heard a familiar voice.

"I hear this place is back on the map." It was McQueen! "There's a rumour floating around that some hotshot race car is setting up his racing headquarters here," he said.

The two cars smiled happily at each other.

"YEE-HAW!'

They looked up to see Mater hooting with delight up in the Dinoco helicopter. McQueen had kept his promise.